DISCARD

9/19   3/17   4/14
6/18   2/17   4/14
29   21   15
                2
                2

D1378145

DISCARD

WHAT IS YOUR DOG DOING?

by
MARILYN SINGER

illustrated by
KATHLEEN HABBLEY

RIVERSIDE PUBLIC LIBRARY
One Burling Road
Riverside, IL 60546

Atheneum Books for Young Readers 🐾 New York   London   Toronto   Sydney

Acknowledgments: Thanks to Steve Aronson, Carol Chou, Emma Dryden,
Kiley Frank, and all the other good folks at Simon & Schuster—M. S.

ATHENEUM BOOKS FOR YOUNG READERS
An imprint of Simon & Schuster Children's Publishing Division
1230 Avenue of the Americas, New York, New York 10020
Text copyright © 2011 by Marilyn Singer
Illustrations copyright © 2011 by Kathleen Habbley
All rights reserved, including the right of reproduction in whole or in part in any form.
ATHENEUM BOOKS FOR YOUNG READERS is a registered trademark of Simon & Schuster, Inc.
For information about special discounts for bulk purchases, please contact Simon & Schuster Special Sales
at 1-866-506-1949 or business@simonandschuster.com.
The Simon & Schuster Speakers Bureau can bring authors to your live event.
For more information or to book an event, contact the Simon & Schuster Speakers Bureau
at 1-866-248-3049 or visit our website at www.simonspeakers.com.
Book design by Lauren Rille
The text for this book is set in Century Schoolbook.
The illustrations for this book are rendered digitally.
Manufactured in China
0311 SCP
First Edition
10 9 8 7 6 5 4 3 2 1
Library of Congress Cataloging-in-Publication Data
Singer, Marilyn.
What is your dog doing? / Marilyn Singer ; illustrated by Kathleen Habbley. — 1st ed.
p. cm.
Summary: Illustrations and simple, rhyming text reveal that dogs do much more than sit, stay, and roll over.
ISBN 978-1-4169-7931-9
[1. Stories in rhyme. 2. Dogs—Fiction.] I. Habbley, Kathleen, ill. II. Title.
PZ8.3.S6154Wh 2011
[E]—dc22
2010016351

To Oggi, who's always doing something
—M. S.

For my mom, Mary; my dog, Gertie;
and my cat, Ginny
—K. H.

Dog dreaming

Dog scheming

Dog inspecting

Dog protecting

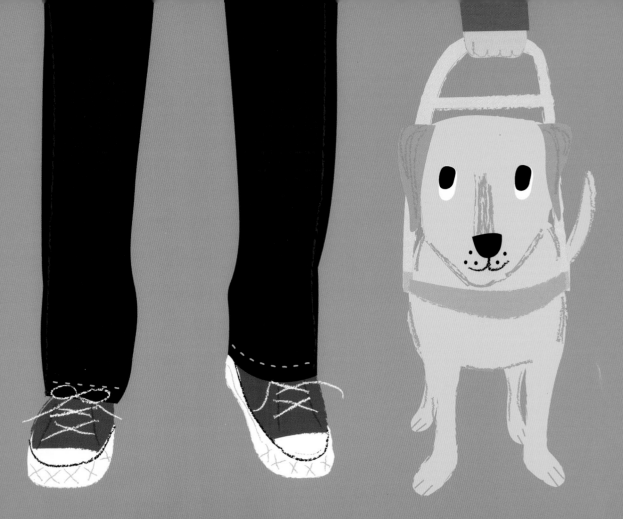

Dog that knows
the way to guide

Dog that knows
just where to hide

Dog sharing

Dog daring

Dog in a chase

Dog in disgrace

Brilliant dog

that loves to herd

gets chauffeured

Dog shedding

Dog sledding

Dog paddling laps

Dog dancing? Perhaps!

Dog that works

the circus tent

Dog that's with the president

Dog wired

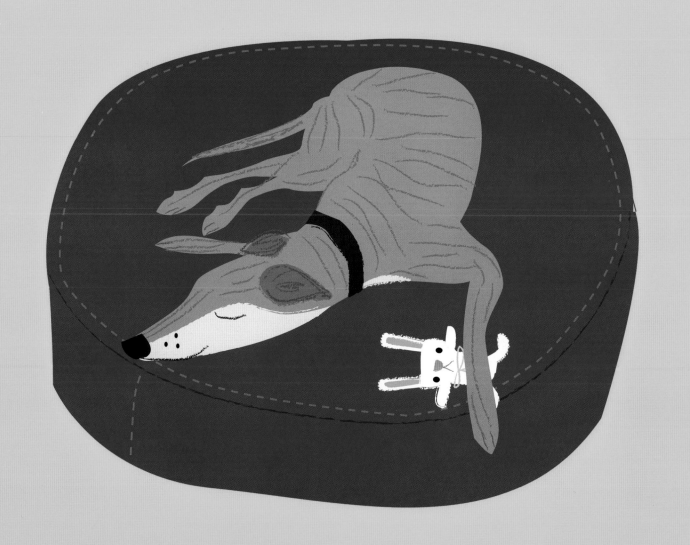

Dog tired

Dog snug in a purse

Dog quite the reverse

Dog laughing

Dog chewing

Tell me,
what is
your
dog doing?